BRATZ™

Pop Princesses

© MGA

Meet the girls!

Yasmin™
a.k.a
Pretty Princess
© MGA

Phoebe™
a.k.a
Sugar
© MGA

Sasha™
a.k.a
Bunny Boo
© MGA

Cloe™
a.k.a
Angel
© MGA

Jade™
a.k.a
Kool Kat
© MGA

Used under license by Penguin Young Readers Group,
Published in Great Britain by Ladybird Books Ltd 2006
80 Strand London WC2R 0RL
A Penguin Company

10 9 8 7 6 5 4 3 2 1

Printed in China

LADYBIRD and the device of a ladybird are trademarks of Ladybird Books Ltd

A regal story told in five superb sections!

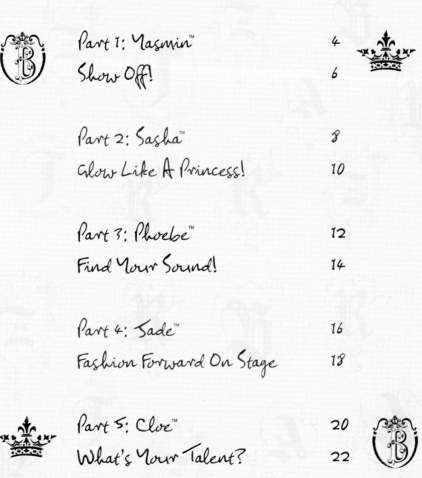

Part 1: Yasmin™ 4

Show Off! 6

Part 2: Sasha™ 8

Glow Like A Princess! 10

Part 3: Phoebe™ 12

Find Your Sound! 14

Part 4: Sade™ 16

Fashion Forward On Stage 18

Part 5: Cloe™ 20

What's Your Talent? 22

Yasmin™

I looked around at the *Stiles Shout Out* office. The holidays had been groovin', and now I couldn't wait to get back in the writing seat and start tapping out some perfect prose for the coolest school mag ever! I had just sat down in front of my computer when the door was flung open and Cloe charged in. I could see at a glance she was in full drama queen mode!

© MGA

"Chill out, girlfriend!" I said, spinning around in my chair to face her. "What's the buzz?"

Cloe flung her sassy new backpack down and sank into the chair opposite me, fanning herself with a leaflet.

"You'll never believe it!" she squealed.

"Believe *what?*"

"This is the most royally cool news I have heard all year!"

"Angel, *what news?*" I said loudly. She didn't seem to hear me.

The door burst open again and Sasha strode in. "The entire school is flipping out," she blurted. "This is the most superb idea ever and I know we are in with a chance – *better* than a chance 'cuz we're already..."

"Bunny Boo, take a breath and..."

The door flew open again to reveal Jade and Phoebe. "Fabulous news!" Jade declared.

"*I am gonna lose it if you guys don't spill the news right now!*" I hollered.

Sasha grabbed the leaflet from Cloe's hand and shoved it under my nose.

"Calling all pop royalty," I read. "This year's prom is gonna be the hippest yet. We're holding auditions all term for the hottest musical entertainment. The winning group will be crowned Pop Princesses or Princes... and will perform at the prom! Anyone can audition – our crack team of judges will narrow the field from there!"

I let the leaflet flutter to the floor as I squealed, "This is a dream come true!"

Show Off!

If you're gonna organise a totally fabulous talent show, you've gotta make a plan! There are loads of things to think about, so here's our guide to ticking all the boxes and making your show a huge success!

Schedule like Sasha!

I know we kinda tease Sasha about being a control freak, but sometimes it's really cool to have a plan! Fill out this schedule sheet for your event and make sure you know when everything is supposed to be happening!

Venue .... My house.

Date .... on a satday.

Start Time .... 7:00am PM

Finish Time 1:00am

Interval ....

Judges' Decision Time! ....

Refreshments ....

Acts

1. ....

2. ....

3. ....

© MGA

The Venue

Where are you gonna hold your show? Whether it's your school hall or a youth club, turn it into a star-studded venue that's full of sophisticated glam. Use rich, royal colours like red, purple and gold.

The Acts

You can't have a talent show if you don't have any acts! Ask all your friends to do something – whether it's a big show-stoppin' number or a chilled-out guitar solo. Decide the order they're gonna appear in and don't put similar acts next to each other – give everyone a chance to shine!

The Judges

Pick three people whose judgement you totally trust. Set up a long table for the judges to sit behind and cover it with a red cloth. Put plenty of water jugs and glasses out for them and give them pencils and paper to make notes. After all the performances have been seen, bring the head judge up on stage and ask them to announce the winner!

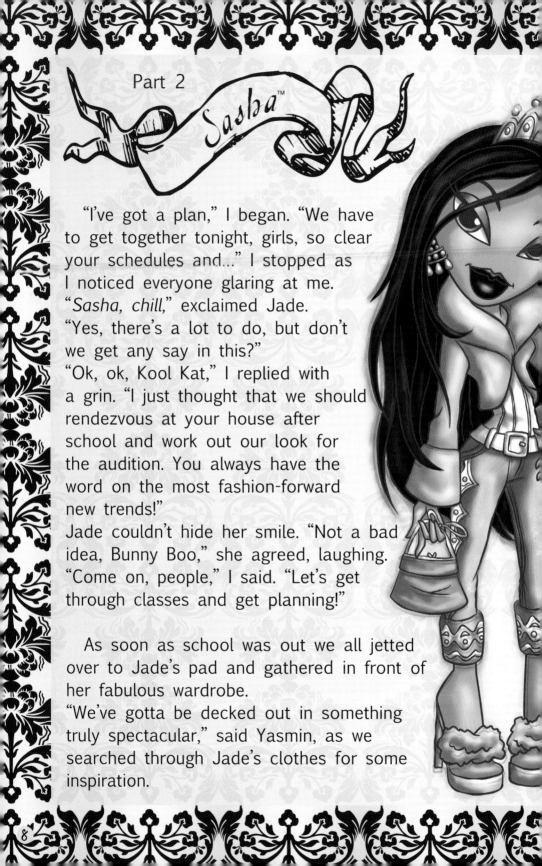

Part 2

Sasha™

"I've got a plan," I began. "We have to get together tonight, girls, so clear your schedules and..." I stopped as I noticed everyone glaring at me.
"*Sasha, chill,*" exclaimed Jade.
"Yes, there's a lot to do, but don't we get any say in this?"
"Ok, ok, Kool Kat," I replied with a grin. "I just thought that we should rendezvous at your house after school and work out our look for the audition. You always have the word on the most fashion-forward new trends!"
Jade couldn't hide her smile. "Not a bad idea, Bunny Boo," she agreed, laughing.
"Come on, people," I said. "Let's get through classes and get planning!"

As soon as school was out we all jetted over to Jade's pad and gathered in front of her fabulous wardrobe.
"We've gotta be decked out in something truly spectacular," said Yasmin, as we searched through Jade's clothes for some inspiration.

"The competition's gonna be *intense*."
"You're so right, Pretty Princess,"
Cloe replied, trying on a beret in
front of the mirror and posing
absentmindedly.
"That's it!" exclaimed Jade.

Cloe took the beret off and
shook her head.
"Uh-uh, I don't think French chic
is quite the look we should be
going for."
"Not the beret!" cried Jade,
throwing it back into her
wardrobe. "Pretty Princess!"
"Yes, that's – my –
nickname," Yasmin reminded her
slowly.
"*Princess*!" repeated Jade. "Listen,
we are gonna be exactly what
the leaflet said. If they want pop
princesses, then that's what they're
gonna get! We'll be the most
royally rockin' band ever!"
"Totally!" exclaimed Phoebe.
"With regal accessories..."
"...and a sound that'll make
everyone bow to us!" I finished.
We were all set to be the
reigning princesses of
Stiles High!

© MGA

9

Glow Like A Princess!

A true princess sparkles with confidence — and when you're on stage that sparkle will give you the edge, girlfriend! So make sure your makeup brings out your royally cool attitude!

Eyes

Remember that when you're on stage, the spotlights will be shining on you, so your eye makeup has gotta be strong and vivid to really stand out!

© MGA

© MGA

🦂 Use satiny cream eyeshadow that will brush over your eyelids like silk. Pick smoky blues and greys and sweep a darker shade close to your lash line.

🦂 Define your peepers with a curving stroke of eyeliner and a brush of ebony mascara.

🦂 Finish off with a hint of sparkle mascara in silver or gold.

© MGA

© MGA

© MGA

Lips

Your lips are gonna be pumpin' out some seriously cool songs, so make sure they look super-glam while you're on stage!

- Use lip balm every day to keep your pout soft.
- To keep your colour in place, first coat your lips with a lip base.
- Apply your lip colour, blot with a tissue and then repeat.
- Finish off with a transparent gloss to make your lips shine!

Skin

To get that royal glow, don't forget to cleanse and moisturise every night and morning. Protect your skin from extreme weather and use a face mask once a week.

- Brush your cheeks with a rose-coloured blush and dab some highlighting cream on your cheekbones.
- Fairy dust your face, shoulders and arms with sparkling face powder!

Hair

Your hair is your crowning glory, so treat it like the crown jewels! Use a deep conditioning treatment once a week and hit the salon for a trim every six weeks.

- Decide how you're gonna style your hair before the night of the show and practise it a couple of times.
- Use a shine serum or glossing spray.
- Finish off your style with tiny flower studs, jewelled hairpins or a princess tiara!

© MGA

Part 3

Phoebe™

Next day we hit the mall lookin' for some posh trends and royal inspiration. "Check out this majorly magnificent skirt!" exclaimed Kool Kat, trying on a frilly black mini that was totally glam.

"You're a total modern-day princess!" said Sasha. "I'm thinkin' lil' tiaras and lots of glitz," added Cloe, framing Jade with her fingers as if she were on the cover of a magazine.

We cruised the boutiques, searching out dazzlin' styles that we knew would help us snag the gig. At lunchtime we saw Cameron and Dylan heading our way.

"You ladies been hittin' the boutiques again?" teased Dylan, noticing all our bags.

"We've been putting together our look for the audition," Yasmin explained.

"Shh, Pretty Princess!" hissed Sasha. "We don't want to spill our secrets to a *rival band*!"

"*What*?" we gasped.

"Yeah," Dylan confirmed, sounding smug. "We're puttin' together a Boyz band that'll rule the school!"

"Newsflash!" Sasha exclaimed. "With our band on the scene, you guys shouldn't be so sure of yourselves!"

"Oh really?" prodded Cameron, folding his arms. "So give us a blast of your sound."

"That's classified information," Yasmin bluffed quickly. We hadn't even thought about the songs yet!

"Fine," said Dylan. "But you've got a challenge ahead if you want to beat me, Cameron and Eitan. Our sound is gonna blow the competition away!"

Dylan and Cameron strolled off and Cloe hid her head in her hands.

"This is a disaster!" she cried. "We haven't got a single song or any lyrics!"

"We need someone who can create a hip new sound!" said Phoebe, looking at Bunny Boo. "Ready to work on some dazzlin' tunes?"

"You got it," agreed Sasha. "But we need words too, Pretty Princess – I hope you're feelin' inspired, girlfriend!"

Find Your Sound!

There are so many awesome types of music that I never get tired of listening to new sound. Everyone has a different fave type of music – even if it changes every week like Cloe's! Here are some of our top sounds – whose CD collection would you wanna borrow?

Jade gets down with girl-power pop.

Yasmin grooves to funky R&B with a global beat.

Phoebe struts to sweet love songs!

Make the Perfect Mixed CD!

A mixed CD is totally awesome for your personal stereo. But remember, it's gotta be a good mixed CD! Here are some tips to help you put together a totally superb collection!

Sasha™ always gets on the dance floor to hip-hop music!

- Decide what kind of mix you wanna make. Will it be listened to on the way to school, chillin' out at home or working out at the gym? Is it gonna be a selection to relax to, or upbeat tracks to get you ready for a girls' night out?

- Don't pick more than two songs by the same band.

- Pick a theme and a genre of music.

- Keep the CD less than an hour long.

- Design fabulous cover art and write hip liner notes.

- Think of a funny or thoughtful title.

- The last song is super-important. Tie it in to the theme.

©MGA

As our audition day got closer, Cloe had at least three drama-queen emotional meltdowns per day. Sasha went into total overdrive control-freak mode. Yasmin walked around muttering lyrics under her breath. Even I had to work on maintaining my Kool Kat vibe. But at last we had the songs and the words – now we had to put it all together!

"Rockin'!" exclaimed Sasha as the last chord of her solo guitar riff twanged through her basement studio. We had practised for hours every night after school and we were word-perfect – but giving a way-cool performance is about more than just knowing the lyrics! We had to get up on stage and show those judges that we were the pop royalty they were lookin' for!

"We've gotta go to sleep now," said Yasmin, pulling off her guitar and rubbing her eyes. "We need to be totally ready for those judges tomorrow." We huddled and high fived – then scooted home to get our beauty sleep!

"I am so psyched to be here!" whispered Sasha for the millionth time the next afternoon.

We were outside the audition room – there were four other bands auditioning that day and we were last up.

"You guys!" hissed Phoebe. "Look who's auditioning before us!"

Dylan, Cameron and Eitan were swaggering into the audition room.

"Oh my gosh, they look so confident, they're bound to be picked and we won't even get the chance to perform!" Cloe cried.

"Hey, that is not the attitude of a true pop princess!" said Sasha. "Being a princess is all about never bowing to the pressure – and knowing that we totally rule!"

"We so do!" I exclaimed, jumping up beside Sasha.

"Totally!" Cloe joined in.

"We rule!" we all cheered in unison.

When the boys came out they were grinning.

"We put in one tight performance!" Dylan told us.

"We'll just have to go one better then, won't we?" said Sasha.

© MGA

Fashion Forward On Stage

Check out the sizzlin' separates we found for our pop prom performance!

Sparkling tiara

Teardrop choker

Flouncy frilly skirt!

Diamond-studded jeans

Pearl-encrusted heels

Ribbon-tie shoes

© MGA

Animal-print jacket

Crown-print tee

© MGA

© MGA

Now it's your turn!

Think about what sort of music you're performing. Are you and your gals rock chicks or blues babes? Design some glam and groovin' styles for your performance!

Style
Queen
♡

Part 5

Cloe™

We went through the doors and saw the panel of judges in front of us. As we took our positions on stage, my legs felt like jelly and I completely spaced. I was gonna forget the lyrics! I was gonna mess up the song! I was gonna fall over on stage! Then Sasha blasted out the first chords and suddenly I was better than ok – because we were on *fire*!

Our audition was fabulous – the combination of our totally hip look and our way-polished sound had the judges groovin' along with us!

© MGA

"Thank you very much," said the head judge. "We have seen lots of great acts – but I can definitely say that you have a spark no one else has shown!"

"Does that mean...?" began Sasha.

"That means," announced the head judge with a big smile, "that you girls are going to be performing at the prom!"

When the day of the prom arrived, we were so psyched we couldn't keep still! The hall was crowded and the décor was regally cool. "And now, it is my very great pleasure to introduce the musical sensation that's gonna rock your night!" announced the head judge. "Put your hands together and get ready to bow to the *Pop Princesses of Stiles High*!"

The lights went down, a spotlight hit us and we launched into our first song! Our glitzy cool pop soon had everyone jammin' on the dance floor! As the lights twinkled on our sparkling outfits we felt like real stars.

In between songs, Cameron came up to us, smiling.

"You totally rock," he said. "This is the hottest dance ever!"

"Even though you guys aren't the stars?" I asked.

"Hey," he replied with a shrug. "We were good – but you are officially pop royalty!"

What's Your Talent?

If your royally cool talents are in a different area, or if you've already had a singing competition, have a variety talent show! Not everyone wants to sing, and there are heaps of other talents and performing arts you can try out! Here are some of our fave ideas!

Play musical instruments

Deck out in classic black, fold your hair into a low chignon and knock out the competition with your regally glam instrumental stylings!

Dance

Whether it's classic ballet or modern movement, put on your dancing shoes and wow the audience!

Comedy routine

People love to laugh, so if you've got a friend who always has you in stitches, give her a microphone and put her on stage!

Gymnastics

If you're a sports fan then use your agility on stage and put on a fab gymnastics display! Back flips, high jumps and some balancing feats will make a super-cool performance.

© MGA

Poetry reading

If you're the sensitive, creative type, give a poetry reading. Make sure you have a great mix of happy, moving and funny poems and you'll keep the audience totally rapt!

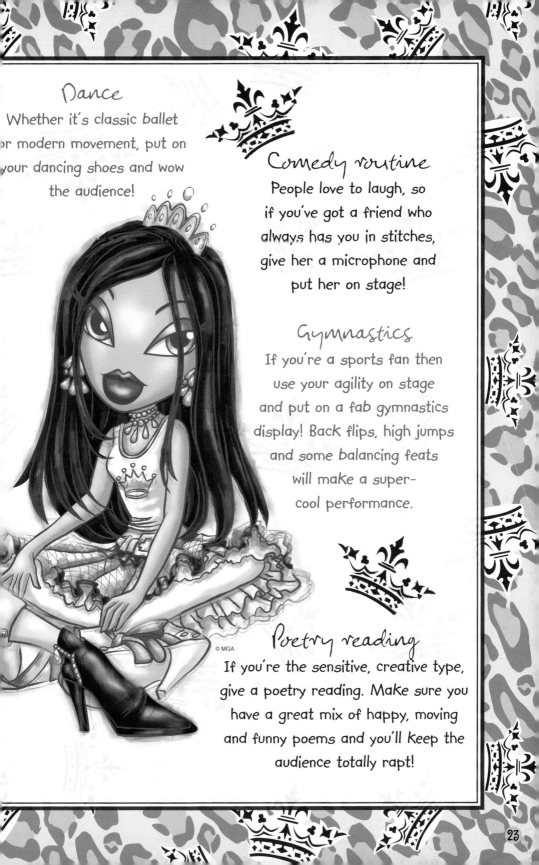

© MGA

Cloe™

© MGA

Sasha™

© MGA

Jade™

We had a superb time performing at the prom and being real princesses for the night! When the spotlight hit the stage we knew that we were born to be stars!

Whatever you decide to do for your talent show, you'll be sure to have a super-glam time with your best friends! Have fun and don't forget – every girl is a princess on the inside. You don't need a castle or a throne – you just need the attitude!

See ya soon!

© MGA

Phoebe™

© MGA

Yasmin™